MCR

JPicture
Fawce.S

Through the Gate

For anyone who has ever struggled with change.

For my family and especially my children, who
I hope will carry the message of this story with
them through the inevitable challenges and changes
of life as they learn and grow.

– S.F.

First published 2017

EK Books
an imprint of Exisle Publishing Pty Ltd
'Moonrising', Narone Creek Road, Wollombi, NSW 2325, Australia
P.O. Box 60–490, Titirangi, Auckland 0642, New Zealand
www.ekbooks.org

A CiP record for this book is available from the National Library
of Australia.

ISBN 978-1-925335-41-5

Designed by Big Cat Design
Typeset in Sabon Roman 18 on 24pt
Printed in China

This book uses paper sourced under ISO 14001 guidelines from
well-managed forests and other controlled sources.

10 9 8 7 6 5 4 3 2 1

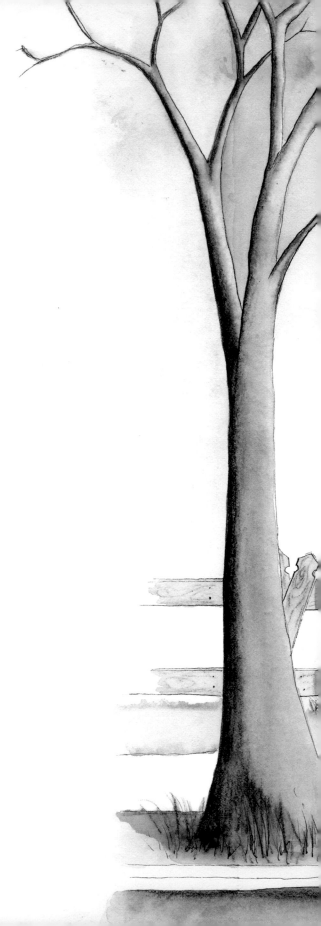

Through the Gate

Sally Fawcett

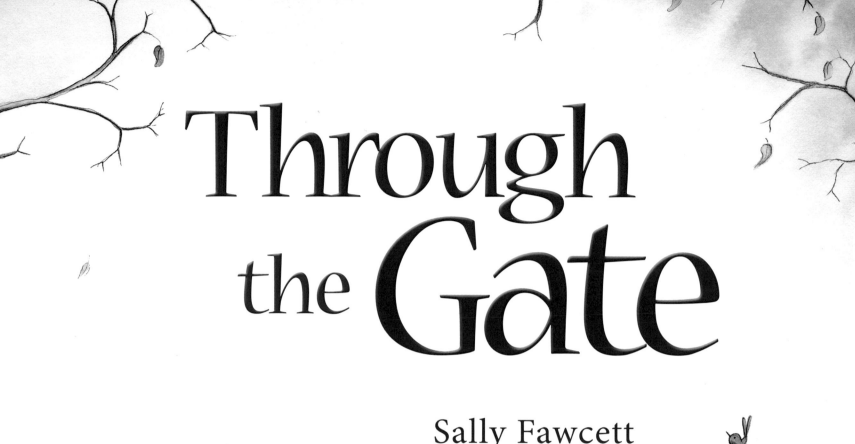

I first saw our 'new' house from the front gate.
It certainly wasn't new.

The roof was drooping.
The paint was peeling.
The step was crumbling.

Everywhere I looked I saw cracks.

I sat on the broken front step of the 'new' house.

New town, new school ... nothing was the same.

I plodded to school ... I plodded home ...

I plodded all week long.

I glared at my shoes and noticed the laces.

My laces had come undone.

On Friday I stopped at our gate.

I glared at the old house ahead.

Something was different.

I mooched to school … I mooched home …

I mooched all week long.

I stared at the ground and noticed some flowers. I picked a few for my mother.

On Friday I stopped at our gate.

I stared at the old house ahead.

Something was different.

I wandered to school ... I wandered home ...

I wandered all week long.

I gazed ahead and noticed a puppy.

I patted him on his tummy.

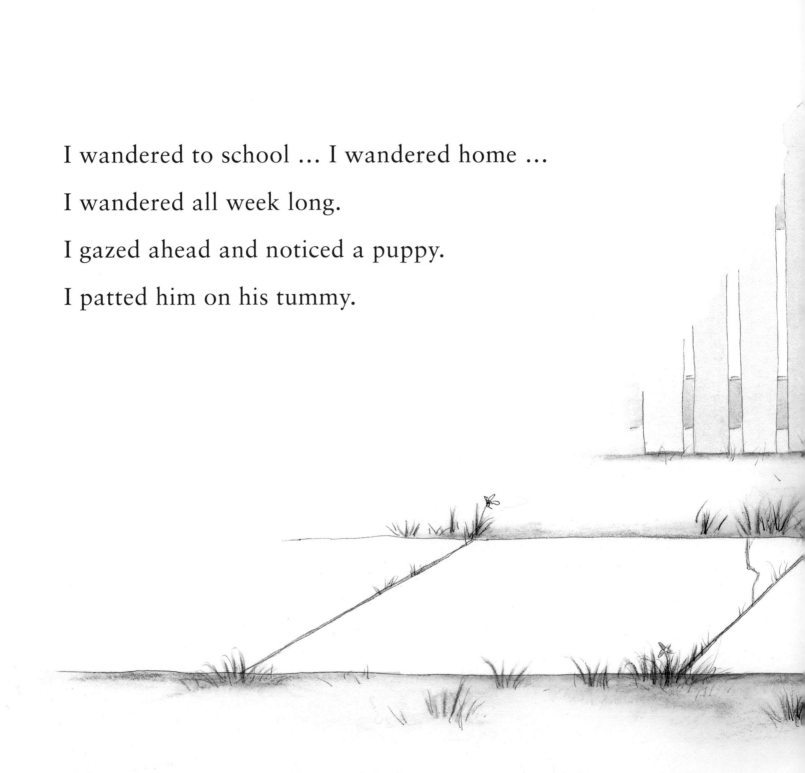

On Friday I stopped at our gate.

I gazed at the old house ahead.

Something was different.

I walked to school …

I walked home …

I walked all week long.

I looked around and noticed a girl.

I invited her to join me.

On Friday I stopped at our gate.

I looked at the old house ahead.

Something was different.

I marched to school …

I marched home …

I marched all week long.

I saw a bird then noticed a tree.

I tasted the sweetest plum.

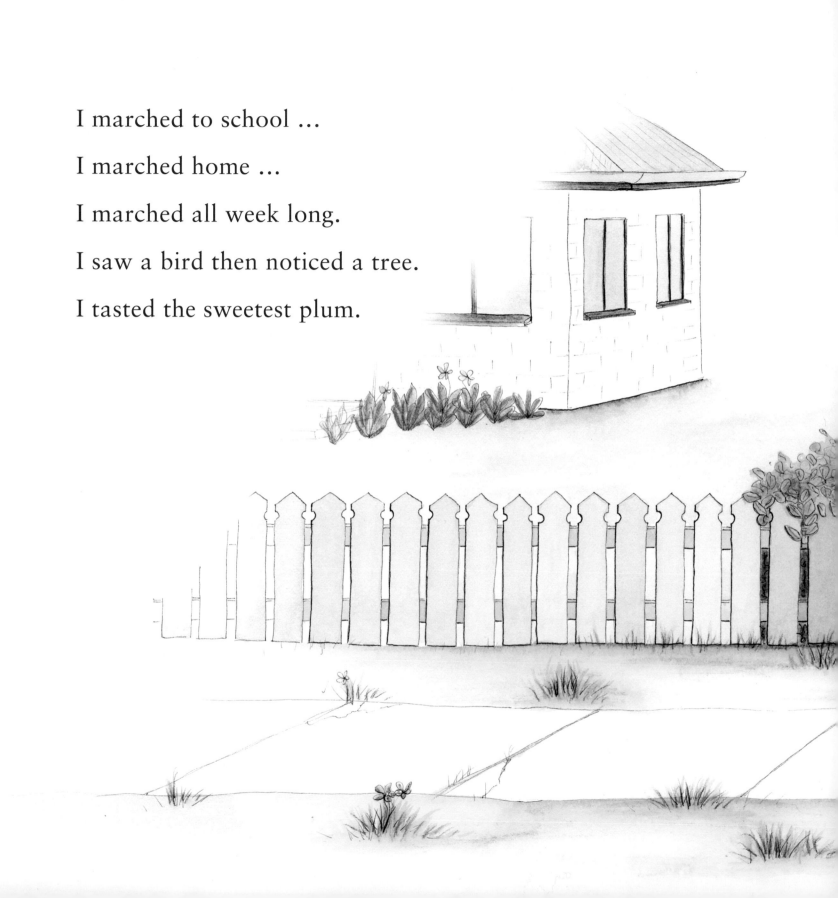

On Friday I stopped at our gate.

I saw our house ahead.

Something was definitely different.

The old house looked new.

How did that happen while I was at school?

Then I felt something else change.

I had a new smile!

I skipped through the gate and into ...

... our home.